ERIC STANTON'S

MY HUSBAND, THE LOSER
LETTER "A"
DON'T PICK UP STRANGERS

Erosetti Press

Let us journey, together

RESTORED EDITION | EROSETTIPRESS.COM
ISBN 978-1-968703-25-7 | COPYRIGHT 2026 EROSETTI PRESS

Introduction to the Three Stories—Restored Edition

Eric Stanton belongs to that rare class of artists who did not merely contribute to a genre, but gave it one of its lasting visual vocabularies. In the 1960s, when underground fetish illustration was sharpening into a fully realized imaginative world of domination, humiliation, leather, heels, posture, and power, Stanton stood at the center of it. His women were not ornaments. They were forces. His men were rarely heroes in the conventional sense. More often they were exposed, corrected, reduced, or absorbed into elaborate dramas of feminine control. Stanton understood, better than almost anyone, that fetish is not only a matter of costume or provocation. It is a theater of hierarchy. It is a way of making power visible.

The three stories gathered here—"My Husband, the Loser," "Don't Pick Up Strangers," and "The Letter 'A'"—belong to that charged 1960s period in Stanton's career, when his art had become both more distilled and more psychologically precise. These are not sprawling narratives. They are concentrated scenarios, each one built around a reversal, an exposure, a humiliation, or a moment in which a man's confidence gives way to a woman's superior command. In them, Stanton does what he always did best: he takes an apparently ordinary premise and turns it into erotic structure. A weak husband becomes the object of ridicule and control. A chance encounter hints at danger, seduction, and entrapment. A single letter becomes the sign of designation, shame, or symbolic reduction. Each story is brief, but none is slight. Each is a chamber of power.

What makes these particular works even more fascinating is the long shadow of Steve Ditko, who is believed to have inked them. That belief is not based on idle fantasy, but on the real creative circumstances of the time. Stanton and Ditko shared studio space for years, and Ditko is documented as having inked some of Stanton's bondage and fetish material during that period. Later reprint metadata connected to this cluster of early Stanton comics also points toward uncredited Ditko involvement. So while the exact line-by-line credits of underground work from this era are often impossible to recover with total certainty, the belief that Ditko's hand may move through these pages is grounded in history, not wishful thinking. That strange overlap only deepens their importance. In one part of the same creative world, Ditko was helping shape the nervous, kinetic visual life of Spider-Man; in another, Stanton was perfecting a private republic of female dominance, erotic humiliation, and theatrical submission.

That conjunction matters. It reminds us that comics history has always been larger, stranger, and more intimate than the official story likes to admit. The border between the underground and the mainstream was never as sealed as later respectability would suggest. Artists shared rooms, tools, deadlines, and influence. They carried one another's line weight, shadows, pacing, and instincts in ways that do not always survive in clean bibliographies. These stories come to us, then, not only as Stanton erotica, but as artifacts from a remarkably fertile artistic moment in New York, when comic-book history and underground fetish history were, quite literally, sharing space.

Yet the true center of this volume remains Stanton himself. Born Ernest Stanzoni Jr. in Brooklyn in 1926, he began with comic-book heroines and professional cartooning, served in the Navy during the war, worked in commercial art, and eventually became the supreme draftsman of female authority in fetish illustration. What made him unforgettable was not simply his subject matter, but his command of form. He understood the eloquence of boots, gloves, corsetry, posture, and restraint. He knew how a woman's stance could establish rank before a word was spoken. He knew how humiliation could be made decorative, how ridicule could be ritualized, how submission could be staged not as accident but as fate. In Stanton, costume is never mere clothing. It is law.

That is why these stories endure. They are not just relics of a hidden past. They are examples of a visual and psychological language that still feels alive. Stanton's themes recur because they touch something deeper than novelty: the thrill of reversal, the ache of exposure, the erotic force of being seen through, classified, corrected, or overmastered. His art gives those tensions form. And in these three compact pieces, we see how efficiently and mercilessly he could do it.

To read Stanton well is to understand that he was never merely drawing kink. He was drawing power as drama, as costume, as punishment, as transformation, and as style. These stories offer that world in miniature. They are sharp, suggestive, humiliating, theatrical, and unmistakably his. And if Ditko's ink indeed shadows Stanton's line here and there, then so much the better: these pages become not only erotic artifacts, but living evidence of a hidden conversation between two artists working at the edge of very different legends.

— Dante Remy | Erosetti Press

STANTON

"MY HUSBAND, THE LOSER"

STANTOONS, INC.
PRUDENTIAL BLDG.
BUFFALO, NEW YORK

ARE YOU GOING OUT TONIGHT..ER.. AGAIN... DEAR? THERE'S SO MUCH WORK AROUND THE HOUSE, I THOUGHT YOU MIGHT HELP!

I THOUGHT I TOLD YOU NEVER TO BELLYACHE IN FRONT OF MY FRIENDS!

PRUDENTIAL BLDG.

STANTOONS INC
BUFFALO N.Y.

JUST HAD TO OPEN YOUR MOUTH IN FRONT OF KAY, DIDN'T YOU? TRY TO MAKE ME LOOK BAD, IS THAT IT?

NO, DEAR, NO!
STANTOONS INC.
PRUDENTIAL BLDG.
BUFFALO, N.Y.

HE'S HAD ENOUGH, BETTE!
LET HIM ALONE BEFORE
YOU KILL HIM!!

DON'T YOU START TELLING ME WHAT TO DO! KEEP YOUR NOSE OUT OF MY AFFAIRS!

WAKE UP YOU CRUMB I WANT YOU TO HEAR THIS!

...AND IF YOU HAVEN'T FINISHED THE ENTIRE HOUSE BY THE TIME I GET BACK, YOU KNOW WHAT WILL HAPPEN!
YES! YES! I KNOW! I'LL.. I'LL TAKE CARE OF EVERYTHING!
STANTOONS INC. PRUDENTIAL BLDG. BUFFALO N.Y.

THE NEXT MORNING...
HELLO, PAUL... KATHY... WHY DON'T YOU COME OVER TO MY APARTMENT!? I THINK IT'S ABOUT TIME SOMEONE TAUGHT YOU THE MANLY ART OF SELF DEFENSE!

THAT WAS FAST, MR. PRENTISS...I'VE SET UP A GYM MAT IN THE PARLOR, SO COME RIGHT IN!
SAID THE SPIDER TO THE FLY!

NOW, PAY ATTENTION, PAUL! THESE ARE THE THROWS AND HOLDS YOU'RE GOING TO USE ON BETTE, SO YOU CAN BE THE MAN AROUND THE HOUSE!
I APPRECIATE THIS KAY, CAUSE I REALLY WANT TO LEARN HOW TO.....
STAN TOONS
PRUDENTIAL BLDG.
BUFFALO N.Y.

LESSON NUMBER ONE, HANDSOME! YOU CAN'T BEAR-HUG WITH YOUR WIFE BE-CAUSE SHE'S TOO STRONG FOR YOU!
CHOKE! CASP

SO, YOU'LL HAVE TO COUNTER WITH A FRONT NAKED CHOKEHOLD...
...THEN SNAKE YOUR RIGHT LEG AROUND HER LEFT LEG AND PUSH FORWARD LIKE THIS!

THE IDEA IS TO GET YOUR OPPONENT ON THE MAT FAST WITH YOU ON TOP, LIKE THIS! THEN REST YOUR WEIGHT ON YOUR OPPONENT'S STOMACH AND CHEST... GRAPEVINE BOTH HER LEGS... LEAN FORWARD AND.. OW! LET GO OF MY HAIR!

OOH! OW! O.K. I GIVE UP!! UNCLE! LET ME UP!
N..O.. NO!
PLEASE, KAY! THAT'S ENOUGH LESSONS FOR TODAY! I DON'T WANT TO GET HOME TOO LATE! BETTE WOULD KILL ME! 
PLEASE LET ME UP! PLEASE LET ME UP!...YOU MAKE ME SICK! (SPAT)
STANTOONS INC. PRUDENTIAL BLDG. BUFFALO, N.Y.
PFFT

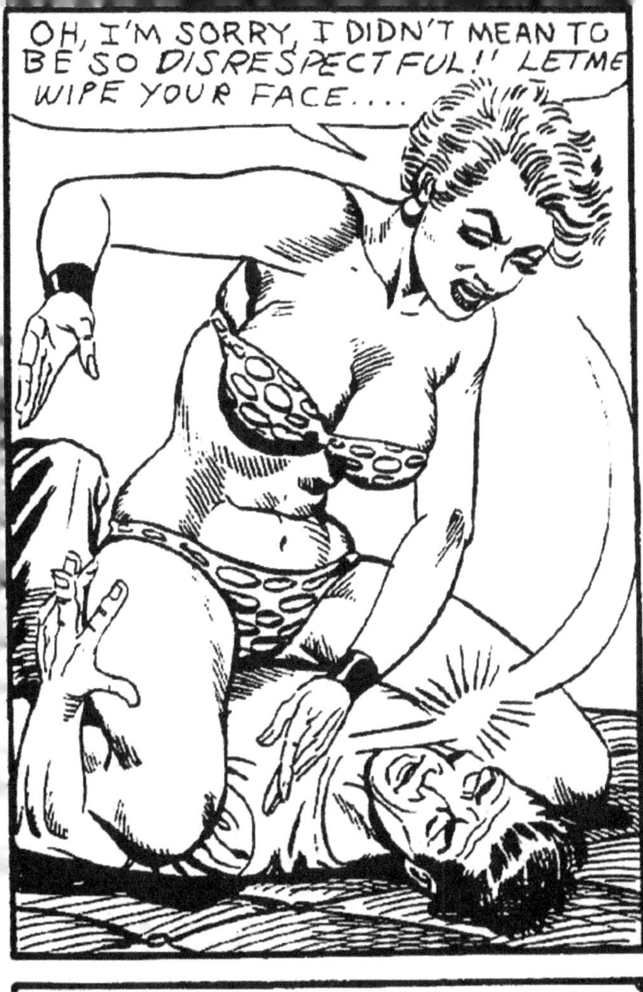

OH, I'M SORRY, I DIDN'T MEAN TO BE SO DISRESPECTFUL!' LET ME WIPE YOUR FACE....

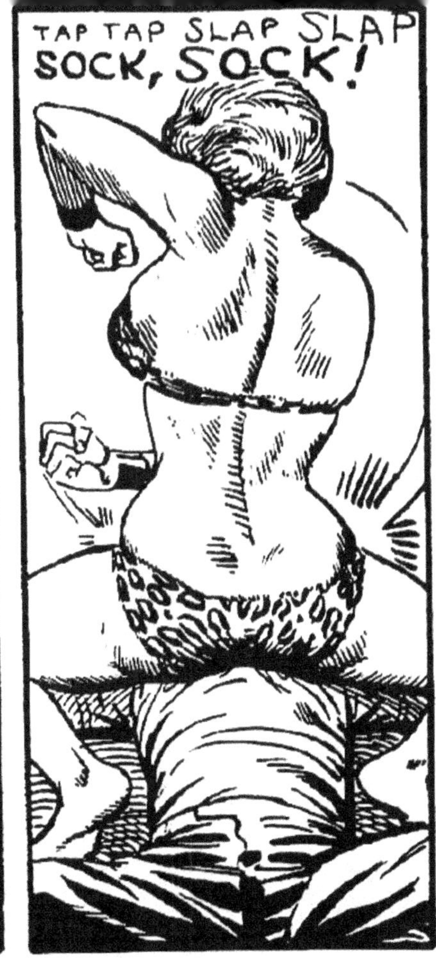

TAP TAP SLAP SLAP SOCK, SOCK!

OHH! YOU HAVE A NOSE BLEED... ...LET ME APPLY A TOURNAQUETTE!
CHOKE! GASP! KAY PLEASE! I... I'VE HAD ENOUGH!!

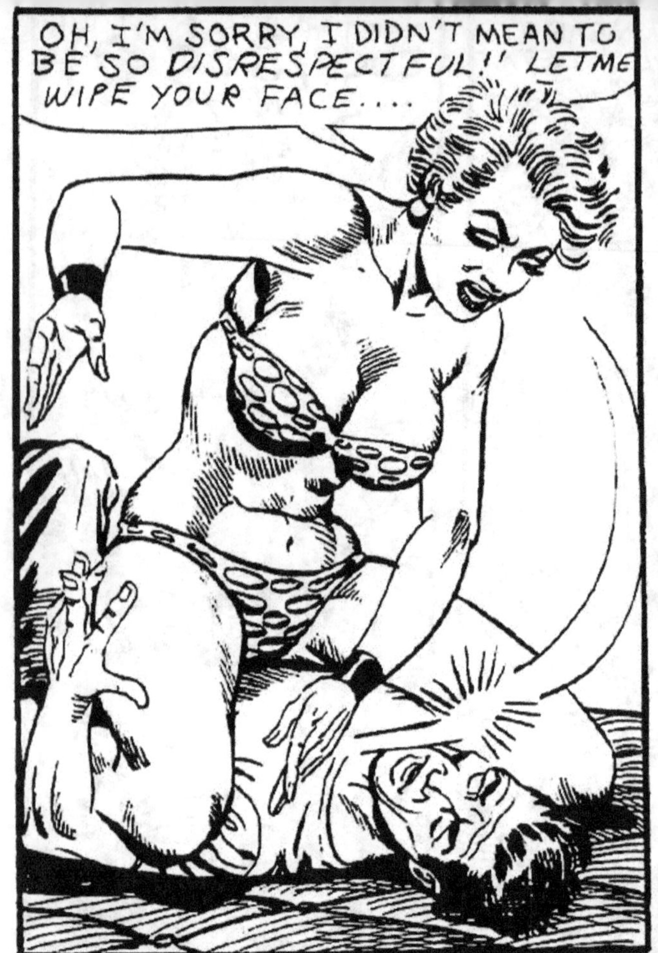

OH, I'M SORRY, I DIDN'T MEAN TO BE SO DISRESPECTFUL!' LET ME WIPE YOUR FACE....

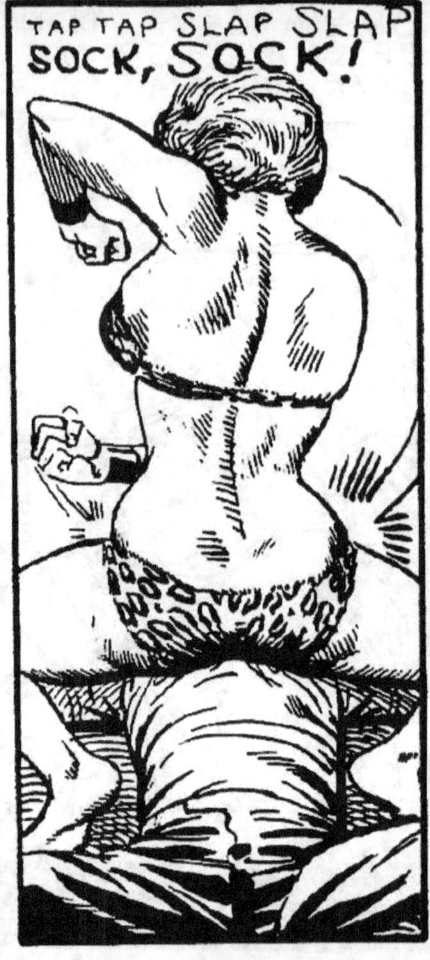

TAP TAP SLAP SLAP SOCK, SOCK!

OHH! YOU HAVE A NOSE BLEED... ..LET ME APPLY A TOURNAQUETTE!
CHOKE! GASP! KAY PLEASE! I... I'VE HAD ENOUGH!!

YOW!! STOP BITING MY LEG!

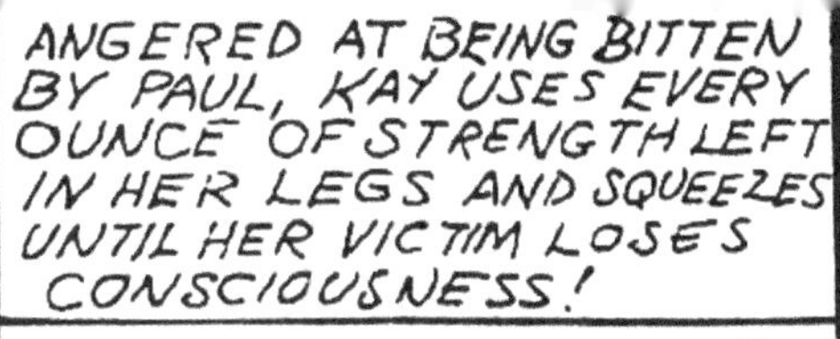

ANGERED AT BEING BITTEN BY PAUL, KAY USES EVERY OUNCE OF STRENGTH LEFT IN HER LEGS AND SQUEEZES UNTIL HER VICTIM LOSES CONSCIOUSNESS!

THE NEXT DAY...
WELL, NOW, GOOD MORNING, SLEEPING BEAUTY! I TRUST YOU HAD A GOOD NIGHT'S REST??
OOH! MY HEAD!.. WHERE.. WHERE AM I?

SO THAT'S WHERE YOU WERE ALL NIGHT!.. HELP ME GET DRESSED, PAUL! I'VE GOT A FEW THINGS TO SAY TO THAT...

"STUPID MUTT! WHEN I
SAY HEEL I MEAN CLOSE
HEEL! KISS MY HEELS! OR
DO YOU WANT SOME MORE
OF THE WHIP?"

TRAINING
YOUR
DOG
by
STAN

GULP!
HA! HA!
CLICK!
POP
2

HA HA HA HA
POW
STANTOONS
PUFF!
PUFF! PUFF!

HA!
AWWK!
CA
FO

HMMMM !!

HMMPH!
RAP!

TSK!
TSK
TSK!
PUFF! UGH!
UGH!
UGH!

GGRRR!

UUUUHH
AAAAHAH! UGGH!
TSK!

AAK
AAK
AAA...
UGH!
UGH!

GRRRRRR
POOOOFFF
AAWK!

..AAA
AAAAA..
UKK!

PUFF!
UH!
PUFF!
UH!
PUFF!
PUFF!
UH!

Dear Sir,
   Since you welcome correspondence I thought I might ask you to offer advice concerning my problem with a very attractive, athletic female.
   I met Helen several months ago and we hit it off handsomely right at the start. We liked the same things, shows, dancing and sports. The latter subject is my forte, or so I thought, until my bragging prompted Helen to challenge me.... Confidently I arrived at her home to prove my allegations. Needless to say Helen beat me badly at the games I boasted about mostly, billiards, tennis and bowling. My pride was dented considerably but I smiled my way through the day of defeat by flexing my muscles and showing my manly physique as often as possible.
   I proved my brute strength to her by losing two hand wrestling matches out of two... Confused and frustrated I challenged her to a no holds barred wrestling battle. Smugly she accepted and began to disrobe.   I cleverly acquired the first hold of our contest but it was my last. Helen put me through a session of the most painful and embarrassing moments of my life. I actually was no match for this Tigress. Her legs were all powerful and that combined with her knowledge of the womanly art of self defense soon had me pinned flat and begging for mercy.
   I love this girl very much and have thought about marriage. What advice can you give me?
                              Sincerely,
                              George F. W.

Dear George F. W.
   Helen needs to meet a man who can defeat her in all the categories you mention. I don't mean blow my own horn, George, but I happen to excel in these events.
                              Your friend,
                              Stanton

Don't Pick up Strangers!

Dear Stantoons,

Your serials are great and the letters from your correspondents have been very interesting -- but I think a recent adventure of my own can put them all to shame. I hope you will use this story for one of the illustrated letters.

Last May, after having spent a few days vacationing in Las Vegas, Nevada I was motoring back home to California. I was alone. Ordinarily I don't pick up hitch-hikers but just past the state border I saw two young women, a blonde and a brunette waving for a lift. They seemed about 22 years old and well dressed in a sort of college style, so I didn't see any harm in stopping to pick them up.

It didn't take long for me to realize I had made a mistake. I had hardly finished asking them where they were heading when Lynn, the brunette, pulled a revolver from her handbag and put the muzzle behind

"THAT'S ALL, LYNN... ONLY TWO DOLLARS"
"LOOKS LIKE YOU GIRLS MADE A MISTAKE!"
YOU MADE A MISTAKE JACK-ASS.."

..PICKING US UP!"

"I SAID, LEAVE HIM HERE!"
BUT...

"GLUG!"

my neck. She was hard and mean. She told me to pull over and I did. The other girl, Laura was a surprise, though. Even though she was also a thief, she at least didn't go about it with a vengeance. It sounds ridiculous but she seemed like a considerate and sweet girl.

We got out of the car and Laura went through my wallet while Lynn tied my hands together behind my back. She pulled the rope so tight my skin burned. I was becoming afraid at this point. Then Laura announced that there was only two dollars in the wallet. Lynn exploded. She acted as though I had deliberately thwarted her. She swung the gun butt against my head and knocked me down. Believe me I was ready to stay down.

"Let's get out of here," she snapped to Laura.

"You can't leave him here tied up like that," answered Laura. "He'll die of exposure."

Laura started toward me to untie the rope but Lynn stopped her. "Leave him here," she said "or I'll leave you here"

"Don't be mean" Laura retorted and again came toward me. I have never seen a woman react as quickly or as viciously as that Lynn. She was a dynamic bundle of pent up hatred who could not bear to be thwarted. She glued herself against Laura's back and brought her to her knees. But Laura had some tricks of her own. She grabbed two fistfuls of hair and pulled Lynn right over her. Once on the ground the two girls tangled in a series of wild snarling cat-holds. Their legs thrashed together or about one another's heads and fingers snatched at clothing as they rolled over and over. No sense of modesty slowed these girls down.

At one point their interlocked bodies crashed into and over me. Their combined weight crushed the breath from me as they fought for dominance. Lynn's powerful thighs straddled both Laura and myself and as they bounced on me I thought I'd die.

Laura finally bucked Lynn off and they continued their clawing scramble while I was able to regain my breath and watch. Fortunately for me, Laura finally managed to scissor her beautiful legs around Lynn's midriff. She had Lynn gasping and within a few more moments was astride her and beating her into submission. After that she untied me and let me go, a sadder but wiser man. I've never forgotten the lesson I learned that day: Don't pick up strangers!

"OKAY! THAT'S ENOUGH! YOU WIN.. UNTIE HIM!"
GEE.. THANKS FOR SAVING MY LIFE! ER... YOU CAN HAVE THE TWO DOLLARS!